Brown and Blue

Brown and Blue

Shaquana Gaskins

To order additional copies of this book, contact:
Xlibris
1-888-795-4274
www.Xlibris.com
Orders@Xlibris.com
795928

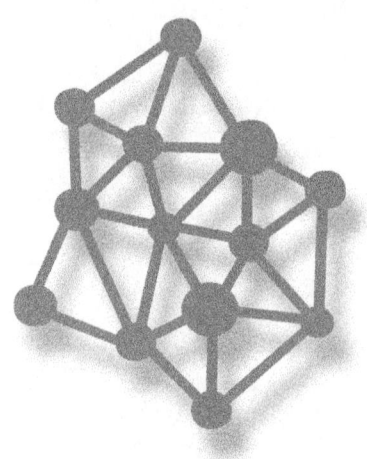

Stereotyping, bad teachings, abuse of power and most of all plain ignorance, are the causes of the common issues we see today. Being a man is already a task but being a black man even harder. You have those who try to down put you arguing everyone is granted the same choices and opportunities but in that argument they fail to mention that different situations can contribute to those opportunities being unlikely to have. No excuses just the truth in its truest form. I know because I'm a product of such situations. Hi, I'm Damarius and I'm proof that what doesn't kill you makes you stronger. The year is 1991, one of the most memorable in my life. West Baltimore Home to many projects. where their are ya middle class folks, the ones barely making it and those living from hour to hour. I was apart of the low class. I

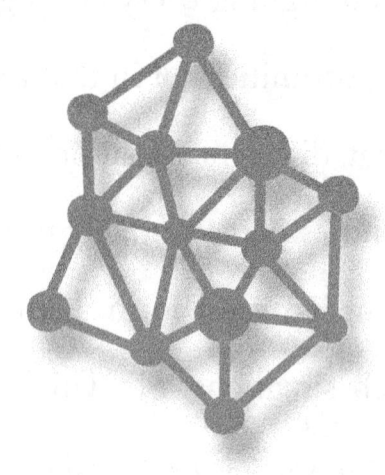

was one of six kids born in a family raised on foodstamps and disability checks. I didn't mind the government handout but that lil chump change they were giving out was barely enough to get us through the month.....that last two weeks was torcher.

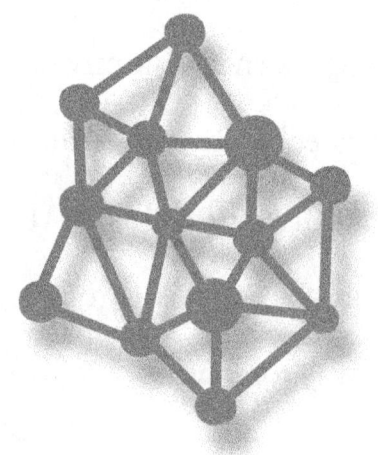

Some days were harder then others but we always made it through and even though drugs consumed her every aspect in life, I loved my mother very much. She hated the fact that I sold drugs and I hated the fact she used them. I guess she was after all worried about me getting hit up on the block. I didn't care I needed the money and it was fast easy and right on time. Where you going Mari? his little sister asked happily as he made his way to the door. out. you can't go so don't ask. he replied. Redwood was my hustle ground everyone knew me and I knew everyone. My man curve was my main right hand man. He looked out for me and I looked out for him. Anybody tryna sound off curve always was the first to know. Yoooo, wassup dummy? Damarius said smoothly. what's good with you? Shit, ready to make some money. Curve replied alright that's what I like to hear. It's jumpin out here today too. For real? Damarius asked... Hell yeah, dummy let me hold ya lighter? curve asked. Aye!!! wassup

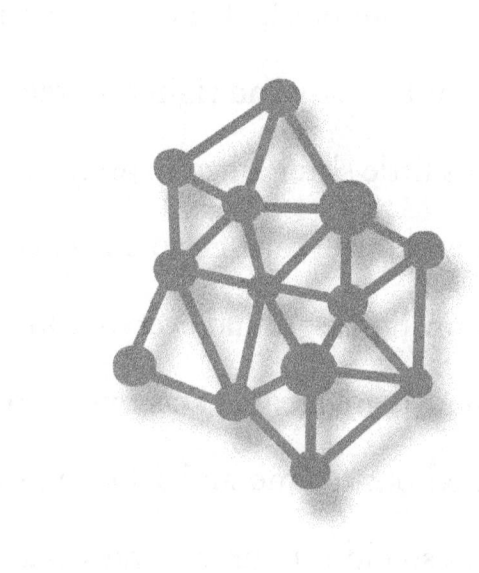

my nigga.....yelled a voice from across the street. Here go

dis snake ass mothafucka. Curved whispered. Vincent

or as I like to call him problem. Vincent was the type of

nigga who was slick out the mouth always played the 50

and always was a half truths nigga.

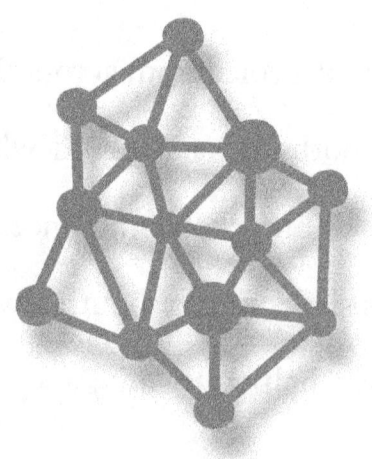

The only reason niggas aint 180 his ass is because his brother was one of the dirtier cops you wanna meet. Vince was famous for getting info, one of his specialties was project hoppin getting the juice on anybody and then using it when it's beneficial to him. He stayed up hillenburg projects and took that info to grand hill projects. Hillen niggas wasn't allowed down Redwood and Redwood niggas put fear in grand hill niggas. Any flashes of green and grand hill was merked vice versa, any flashes of orange and hillen. burg had to be layed down. Me I feared no one I was ready to take a life at any moment. Sorry to be so cold but I felt no consequence was great enough to be feared not even death himself. Even though beef was a common thing among the projects we also had a shared understanding of hating the police. when your a little carcassion boy growing up your taught that police are hero's and they protect you, but when your a little black boy growing up in the projects some are taught the same but our teachings cant hide what the

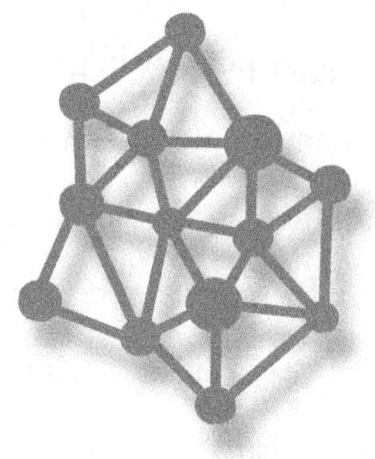

eyes have seen. when I was eleven I witnessed a officer beatup a known gangbanger because he laughed after being arrested. As his partner watched I could tell he wanted nothing to do with the abuse takin place but as a rookie I guess you feel like your word isn't much of a fight.

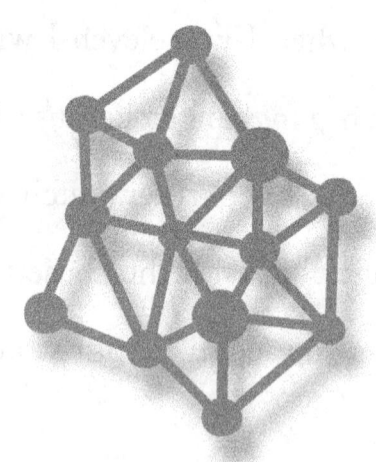

All police aren't bad though like society wants us to believe. Just like any job, church, group, etc, their a few bad apples that ruin the bunch and because of this words like stereotype come into play. This is one of the few reasons why ignorance plague our society today. Dummy you tryna go to the store? Damarius asked curve. Curve said tiredly naw I got a lil bitty I'm tryna holla at tonight. Oh true...Damarius agreed. He walks away in confidence six blocks down Redwood onto Jamison avenue. He enters the store observing the people in their. Hi, Mr Jay he said knowingly. Mr Jay was a well respected store owner who. Looked out for those who needed it. Hey Mari I was just thinking about you. when you going leave that mess alone and make some honest money. Damarius let's out a lil chuckle that life ain't for me Mr Jay, I ain't ready to punch no clock. He walks down the isle patiently looking at the chip bags. The door slams open. what's up old man??? a voice says in the distance. Now I told you

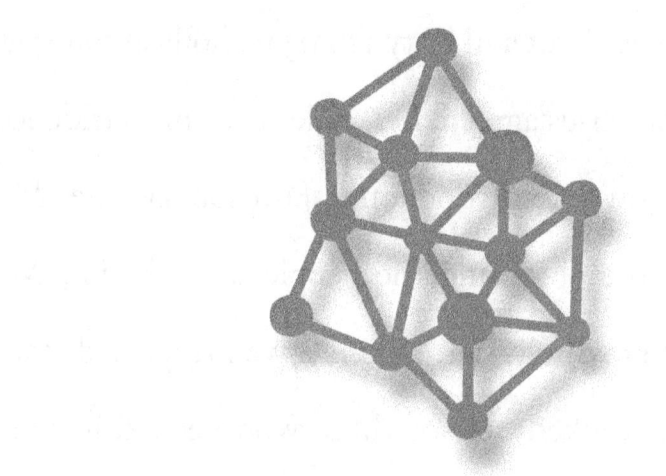

to stay from round here. you ain't nothing but a trouble maker and everyone around you dies. says Mr Jay Stern yet scared. Damarius looks up and observes a average built man. Hanging from his back pocket was a orange scarf. A hillen burg nigga.

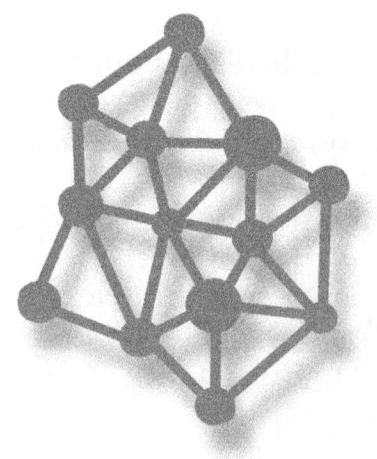

Relax old man me and the homies gonna grab some stuff on you, and we'll be outta here. Damarius slowly moves towards the group of men. Aye I think y'all better do what he says. Tyrell or as he called himself hunter, Chuckle's at the demand being given. So is that suppose to scare me. Damarius slightly turns his head sideways like an owl then punches hunter with a left hook, knocking him into the potato chip stand. Mr Jay let out a laugh of relief. OK, it's funny old man, to let's be out. Hunter says. I'll see you real soon old man. Damarius makes his way back up Rose wood. As he comes up he watches while curve gets out an all black Mercedes. Daaaaaamn!!!! nice ride he says admiring the nice car. well shorty got a lil money. curve replied. Right Right Damarius agreed. As the night fell over the projects the two Sat on the stoop of an old abandoned apartment. Even though the police occasionally road through and warned them off the stoop, that didn't stop them from continuing to make sales.

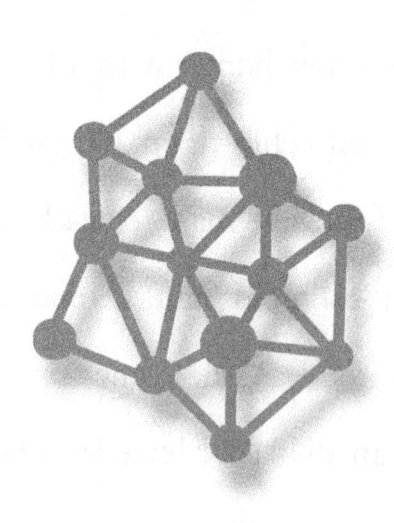

Around nine-thirty, An officer slowly approaches the stoop. Radioing his loud speaker, he yells, "Alright let's break it up time to move it along gentleman. Man I'm bout go back over shorty house curve says. Are catch you later I'm bout to run back I need another rello anyway. Damarius makes his way back down the street towards the store. As he walks, he notices a dark colored vehicle following him. With no fear in his bones he continues to walk rarely even looking back. I'm back Mr Jay. You back again son Mr Jay says. Yep forgot part of my happy kit. He laughs. Do me favor son, watch this her old register while I take out the trash. Mr Jay asks. Aw Mr Jay you trust me that much. Well shoot 27 years of knowing you I better be able to. Mr Jay makes his way to the back of the store. Damarius stands at the counter tapping his fingers and whistling a made up song. He looks out the

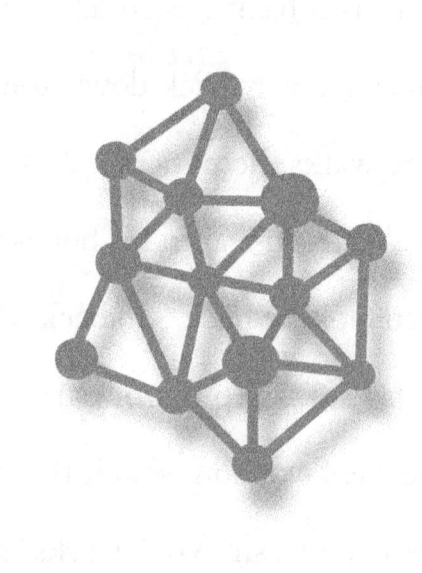

store glass window and notices that a dark colored vehicle was painstakingly passing the store more wondering then worried, he looks around at the ceiling and floor. Dag Mr Jay you taking kinda long. He whispers to himself. He decides to go check out the long winded store owner.

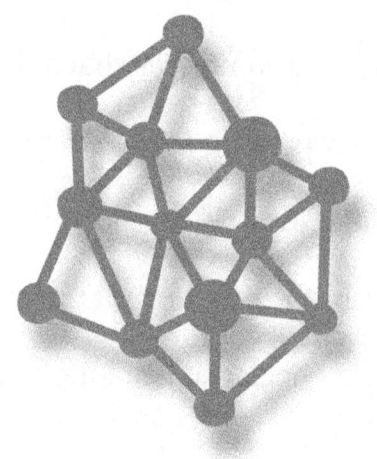

As he makes his way to the back of the store he opens the back door. In that instant a two by four hits him across the face forcing his head to hit the door. A car speeds off then complete silence. Minutes later in pain and confused Damarius wakes up. His vision is a little blurred and then comes into focus. He notices blood all over his gray T-shirt and a six inch blade in his hand. Oddly and scared he looks to discover a body laying in between the dumpsters. He lets out a loud cry. No!!!! Mr Jay No!!! what happened what the...... Heeeeeeelp!!! he screams out in desperation. Near by police arrive at the scene. Sitting in the back of the ambulance, he is approached by a officer. Hi, My name is officer young. He says in his Texas acient. Do you know what occurred tonight son? he asks. Barely able to form words without

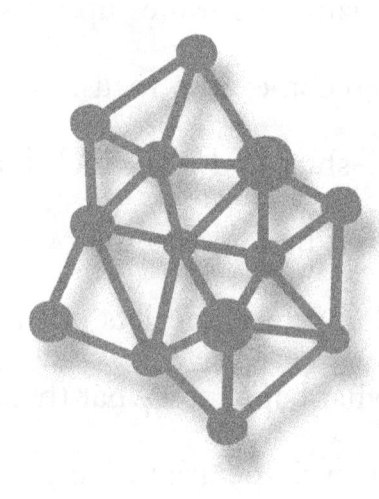

crying, Damarius looks up at the officer and says...I don't know....I really don't know. The officer replies, well since your the only other person besides the victim and he's not talking, imma have to take you downtown and ask you some further questions.

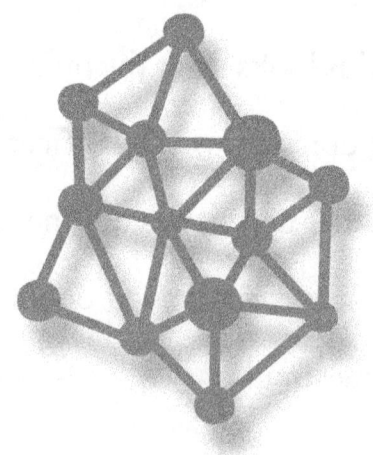

Still confused he agrees to go to the police station. The sirens wale away in the dark like a crying baby. Damarius sits in a cold interrogation room. Still in shock tryna piece together the events that occurred he silently thinks to himself. The door opens and a tall slender gentleman enters the room. Hi my name is detective Tucker and this is my partner detective King. We just wanna ask you a few questions, is that OK? he asks. Yes that's fine. Damarius says sadly. Did you know the victim? asks detective Tucker. Yes his name is Mr Jay and he owns the store.Well do you remember the events that unfolded tonight. Well he exclaimed, all I remember is that I watched the register. Mr Jay took out the trash and then I went looking for him. Everything else is a blurr. Well, I don't believe you says detective Tucker. Your telling me that all you did is watch the store. Yes that's all I did, He said angrily. Detective Tucker slams his hand on the table like a mallet. You have his blood on your shirt, the murder weapon in your hand with only your prints

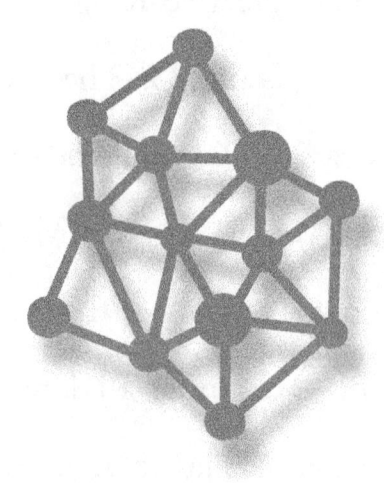

on it and you were the only one present at the time of the murder and you don't know what happened.You did this!!!!! he yelled. I didn't do it!!!! Damarius screamed. Detective!!! I think you should go take a walk. detective King says. Detective Tucker replied, "I'm fine............it's fine. As of right now I'm charging you with murder in the first degree says detective King. You have the right to remain silent any thing you say can be used against you in the court of law. you have the right to an attorney, if you cannot afford one, one will be appointed to you.Do you understand these rights? ? ? .

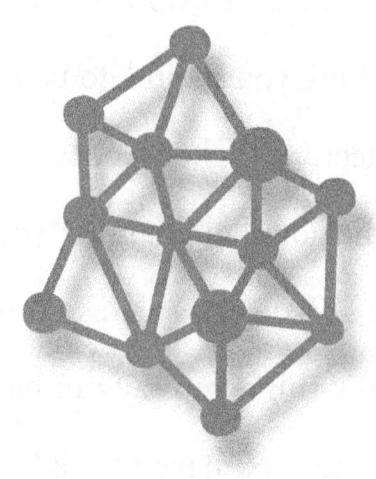

Damarius hangs his head as he is cuffed and booked. Detective Tucker stands next to detective King. So what do you think.....honestly I don't know...I really don't know. Hours later Damarius arrives at Baltimore city correctional facility. After being photograph Ed and thoroughly searched he is taken along with several other images for bunking. Let's move!!!! says officer Clayton. The isle filled with noise as he passed by threats being made, kisses being blown, angry stares filled the air. Freighten on the inside even though he portrayed that tough roll he had never been to jail before. He arrives at his cell. On the top bunk layed his cell mate. A shaggy biker lookin guy with tattoos every where and a long beard. He layed reading his book with his glasses sitting on his nose. You've been a bad booooy. He says teasing Damarius. what's it to you old timer. Relax he says I'm just messing with you.....I'm clyde what's your name? Damarius he replied. Well Damarius you what are you in for? ? ? They say murder but I'm innocent. Clyde

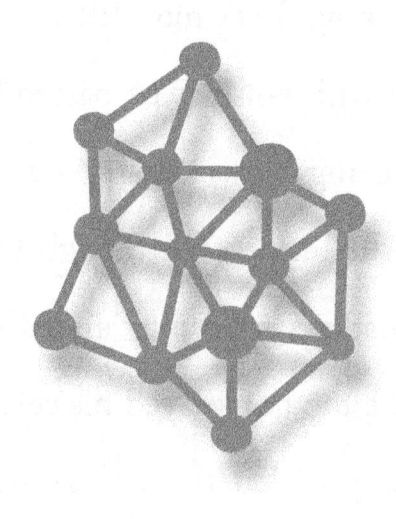

laughs...aaaah well everyone in here claims their innocent. Damarius says aggressively, "well I'm not everyone. Well, son you have no idea what you've done. This is the worst jail to be in. Says clyde. All jails are bad. says Damarius. Yep, clyde exhales but this one is so crooked, even those in power ignore the mess that goes on here.

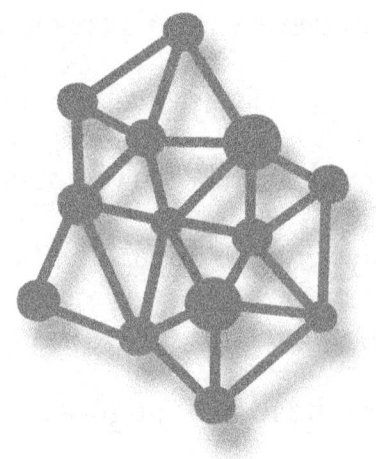

The alarm sounds like an old rusty buzzard. what's that? ? ? Damarius asks clyde. Oh that's the fourth Bell he says.......it's chow time. Damarius gets his food. He looks at it in disgust. Damn!!! all they have is dog food here. observing his surroundings and watching the crown divided amongst groups, he grabbed a seat across from clyde. several correctional officers line the walls of the cafeteria. Now let me explain something to you. I'm the only friend you got in here. Everyone in here is your enemy. says clyde. Damarius says giggling in sarcasm, "and what makes you a friend and not an enemy? . Clyde shakes his head. A enemy wouldn't tell you that right now you in danger and don't even know it. Damarius Chuckle's. Thanks but no thanks I ain't come here with friends and I don't need friends. Clyde silently devours his meal and walks away leaving the cafeteria. As Damarius eats he can't help but notice the putericans watching him. Problem!!!!? he shouts in anger. One guy comes forward. His body filled with tattoos and his head cleanly shaved.

Yeah, I got a problem. I'm in need of some new bitches and your on my recruit list. Damarius gets up standing at 5/9 he was puiny compared to the 6/7 giant. I'm nobodies bitch he says. I'm Santos the guy says, and if I say you are then you are.Damarius throws a punch barely causing pain to his left jaw. Santos punches him in his stomach then slams Damarius on the table. oddly enough while taking a vicious beating he notices none of the guards jump in to help.

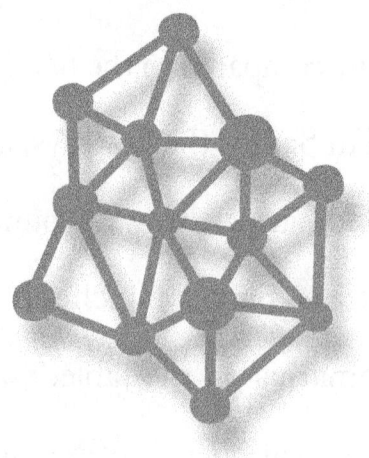

After the vicious attack, he is returned to his cell in pain and agony. Clyde watches in quiet. Now do you see he says gently. What the hell was that Damarius cries out. That was just the beginning of what's in store he says. Clyde hops out his bed and sits next to Damarius. Now let me explain what really goes on in this place. We are all guinney pigs in a fight for survival.One day out of every week to every other week, the people in charge host survival fights. People come from all over to pay big money to see these fights. That's illegal Damarius says. Not when you are in power says clyde. Once one of you win as in leaving the other dead, the winner is rewarded with a shorter sentence and sex with an unwilling female C.O. Damarius could not believe his ears. The night fell over the jail and the last buzzard rings for lights out.He

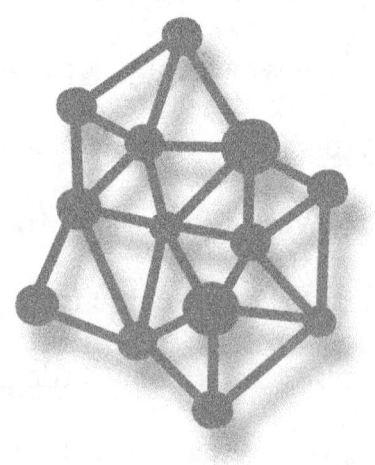

could not sleep, staring into the dark ceiling, pondering what clyde had said to him. Just the thought of such ruthlessness was going on he still couldn't ignore the fact that he was in their for murder and didn't know how or why.

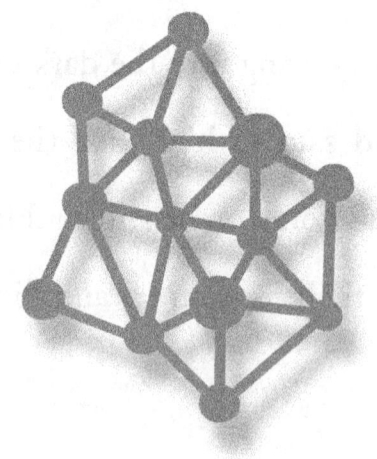

As the night went on morning came pretty quickly. A guard approaches the cell. His voice was deep and Stern. Damarius Thomas? ? , You have a visitor. he says. Damarius was escorted down the hall. Apon entering the recreational room, he sees curve. Aw man wassup Damarius says. Nothing man missing you on the block. how you been holding up curve asks. Man I been surviving, but it's some real messed up stuff going on in here. Damarius gets in to detail about what was told to him. Curve is shocked. Yo man, you gotta say something. I can't Damarius says the guys in power are in on it too. C.OS, the head, hell even the government is in on it. Well we gotta do something to get you out of here. A man on the far end of the room starts acting crazy. Yelling and screaming you can't make me I won't do it. The visit is cut short. The days go by and then weeks. Monday morning Damarius is scheduled to speak with a court appointed lawyer. He watches as the young lawyer comes stumbling in and grabs a seat. Hi I'm Jeffrey Walsh. I'm

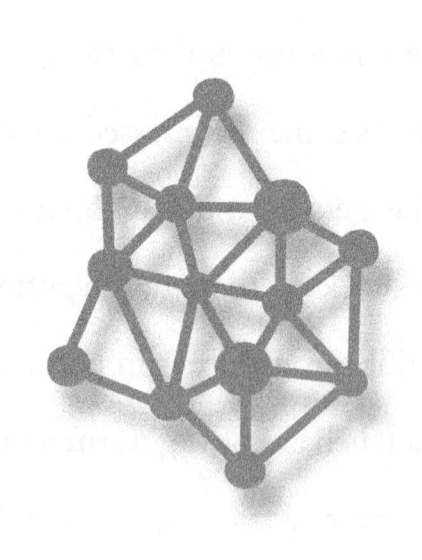

your court appointed attorney how are you. Damarius stares as Jeffrey holds his hand out hoping for a shake. Having the feeling Damarius isn't happy he slowly brings his hand in and opens his brief case. OK let's see, you are being charged with first degree murder. Yea but I didn't do it, Says Damarius. Indeed you didn't but the evidence proves otherwise. So I say we plead guilty at best you'll serve 15 years tops and go on with your life. That way every one wins.

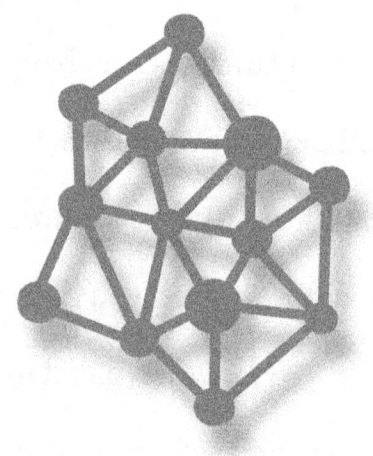

Damarius face turned red. His eyes grew big and his voice low but angry. You walk in here in your fancy Taylor made suit, with intentions to defend me hoping I'd cop to a plea deal so that you can get a win and rest easy at night. You gotta be kidding me. and to add insult to injury brother you ain't even have the decency to ask me my first name. I pity you.... I pity all white collard mothafucka who are in it for the money and publicity rather then the passion and justice for thy fellow man. Well I'm sorry you feel that way.Jeffrey replied. Your fired.I'll have a lawyer by my court date says Damarius. Jeffrey leaves the room. Damarius is returned to his cell. He began his journey of writing letters and reaching out to lawyers with big names in the legal system as well as reaching out to people help for paying his legal fees. Mostly everyone shyed away from helping him not knowing what to believe. Tuesday afternoon, he received a letter from John Moore and associates, one of the most respected names in the business. He began to read the

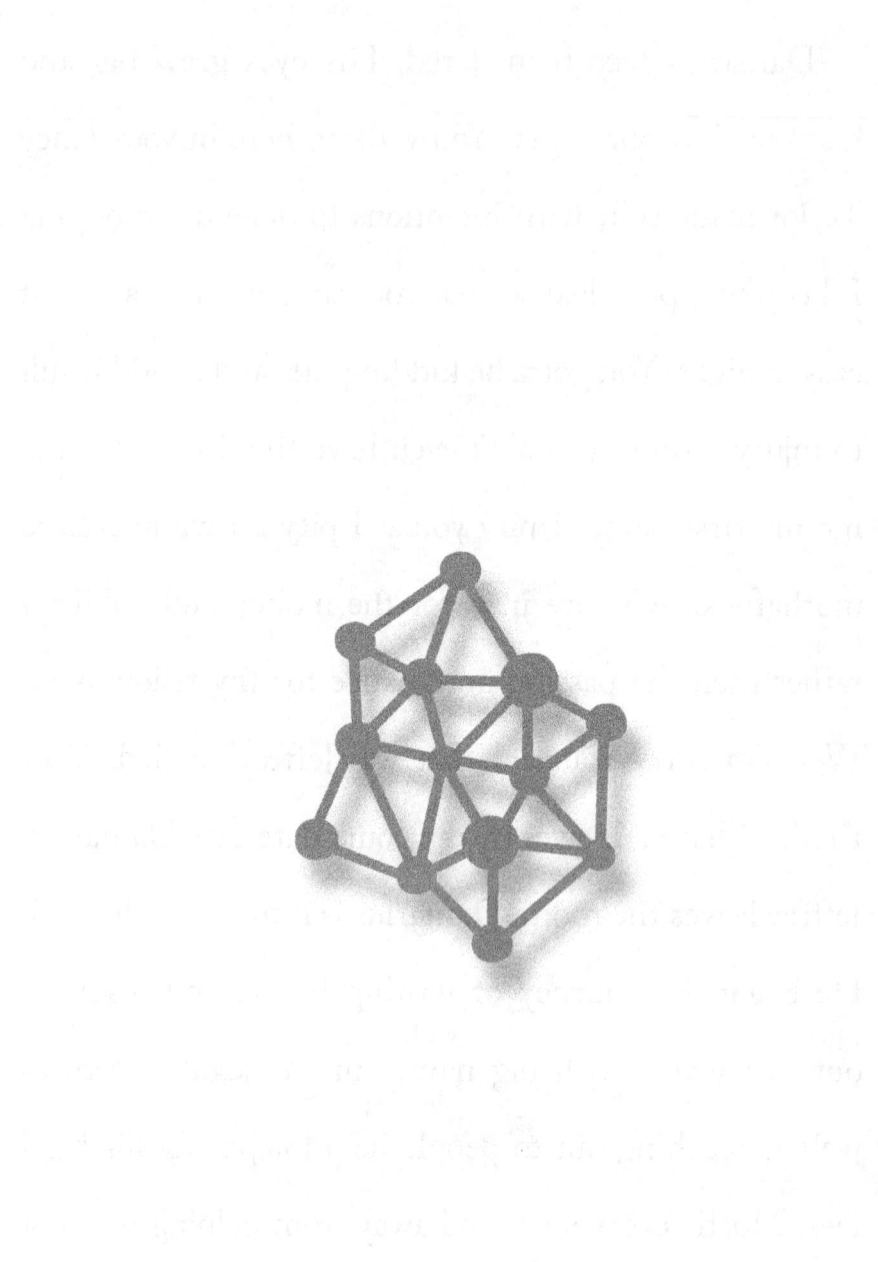

letter with his chest heavy hoping for good news. It read, ;
Hi, my name is John moore and I came across your letter
in the mail. After reading it I have agreed to take on
your case probono. Damarius was relieved and even more
greatful that someone was willing to help. John rides over
to the jail to meet with Damarius. They sit across from
each other in the interrogation room. Hey Mr Moore
Damarius says shaking his hand. Hyd Mr Thomas? he
replied. I'm gonna be honest with you. This is a tough
case. I mean it looks like the defense has an open and shut
case based on the evidence. says Mr Moore. Let me ask
you something. Damarius says. Before we go any further,
Do you believe I did it? . Mr Moore let's out a small
sigh...do you think you did it? ? ? Damarius slouches back
in his chair. I know I didn't, Mr Jay was good to me. I
just gotta figure out how to prove it. I believe in a sense
everyone is innocent until proven guilty.

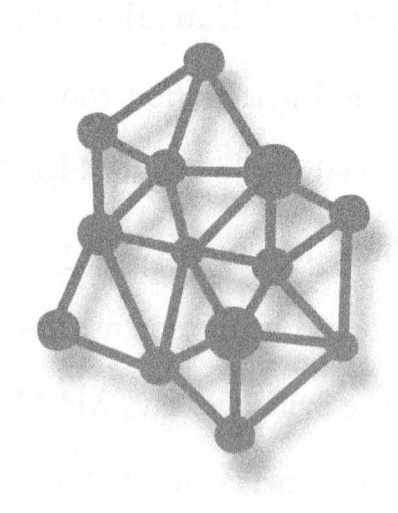

I'll tell you this I'm gonna fight this case to the best of my ability. Even if we don't win, at least we put up a fight. The door closes shut. John goes back to his office at the law firm. A knock on his office door. Attorney Sheila Wyatt enters the room. Aaaaaah another case I see you working on. she says. Yep the Jay Morgan case. he replied. She says with familiarlarity, " I heard about that case. Yeah well everyone seems to think he's guilty...... what do you think? she replied. Honestly I don't know what to think but I'll tell you this, I'm gonna try my best to prove his innocence. And how are you gonna do that? she asked. I don't know yet but it will come to me. Two hours later John revisits the scene of the crime. He slowly revisions how the events may have unfolded as if he were their when it took place. While walking he remembered that in his ten years of being a lawyer that no matter how many times you look over a crime scene their is always the smallest piece of evidence left behind. He grabs his phone and places a call to the corners office. Mr Taylor,

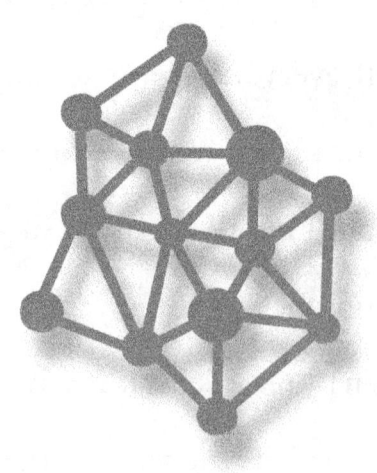

the forensic pathologist answers. Hi, my name is John from John Moore and associates. I was wondering if you could give me a little detail about the autopsy performed on a John Doe turned into you last Friday. Oh sure, Mr Taylor says. Well let's see your victim here had eight stabb wounds. Six to the chest and two to the face. Ironically that's not what killed him. John paused in complete silence for ten seconds.

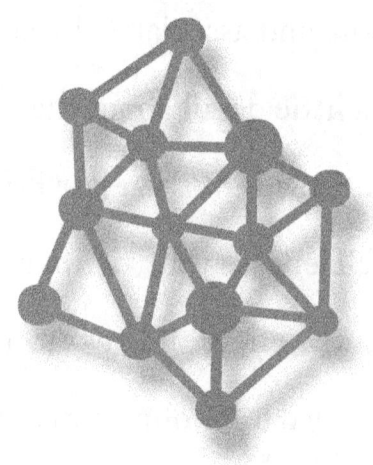

So.....so what killed him? he asked. Although your victim had many stabb wounds none of them penetrated an artery or major organ. What did kill him was a small caliber gun. The 32 shell case went through his heart and exited out his shoulder.

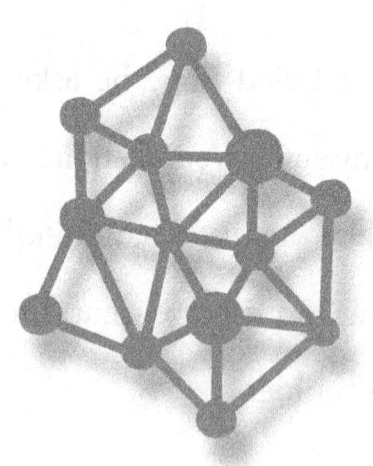

John was in shock. He continued to look around trying to find the bullet. Turing around facing the side street he notices, a tree a playground and a trash can on the other side. He rushes across the street then began to slowly examine the tree. It was perfectly in tack. Then he digs in the trash with a plastic bag over his hand. Then he pulls out a Pepsi can with a hole on the side. After shaking the can and hearing the rattleing. He begans. to smile. This was the evidence he neèded to make his case. Excited about the news he rushes the new found evidence back to the evidence room. Hey!!!, he yells to Taylor. Can you get a rush on the ballistics on that bullet? . Taylor replies I sure can just give me 48 hours to run all possible tests and rule out any inconsistencies. Thanks Taylor, I just hope this bullet tells it all. John makes his way back to the prison. Damarius and he both meet again in the interrogation room. I have some news he says. Damarius stares down at the table. I have some good new...... well aren't you gonna look at me? . Damarius slowly lifts his

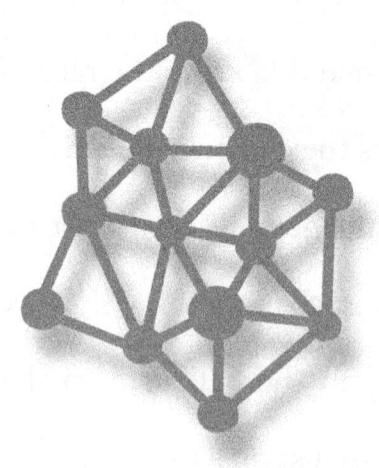

head revealing his swollen lip and black eye. His lip was like a water balloon being squeezed until it burst.Oh geesh! John says. what happened? . Damarius starts to cry out uncontrollably. You gotta get me outta here! if I stay any longer their won't be a trial. John sits back in his chair. Don't worry I'm gonna make some calls, I'm gonna see if you can be moved to a lower secured facility. No, You don't understand he replies this was the work of security.John shakes his head in disgust.

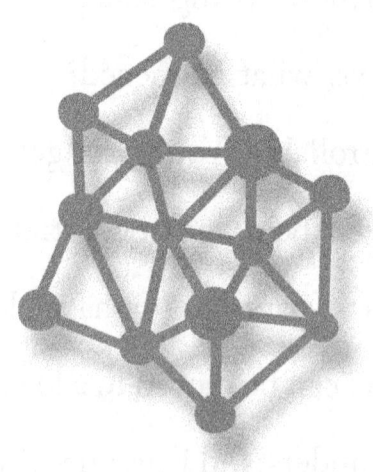

Moments later he goes back to the office and starts making calls. Frustrated that no one would move to transfer Damarius he rubbs his face in grief. He then places as call to defense lawyer lowden. They both meet at a bar on the other side of town for drinks. The two shake hands. John Moore and Terry lowden back on the courts battle field once again. What's wrong? Afraid of the ass kicking your gonna take when we win this case. says John.I'm not the one who should be afraid says lowden. You have no way of proving that your client did not commit the crime. John laughs, " I have the bullet that killed the victim. Lowden straightens upward in his chair. A bullet with no weapon to pin it to, a knife with his bloody prints all over it and a bloody scene pointing all fingers to him....you have squat. In all the years I've known you John I've never heard of you using squat to wina court case. John gets out of his chair angry and aggressively putting on his jacket. You know something you may be right about the evidence and the chances of

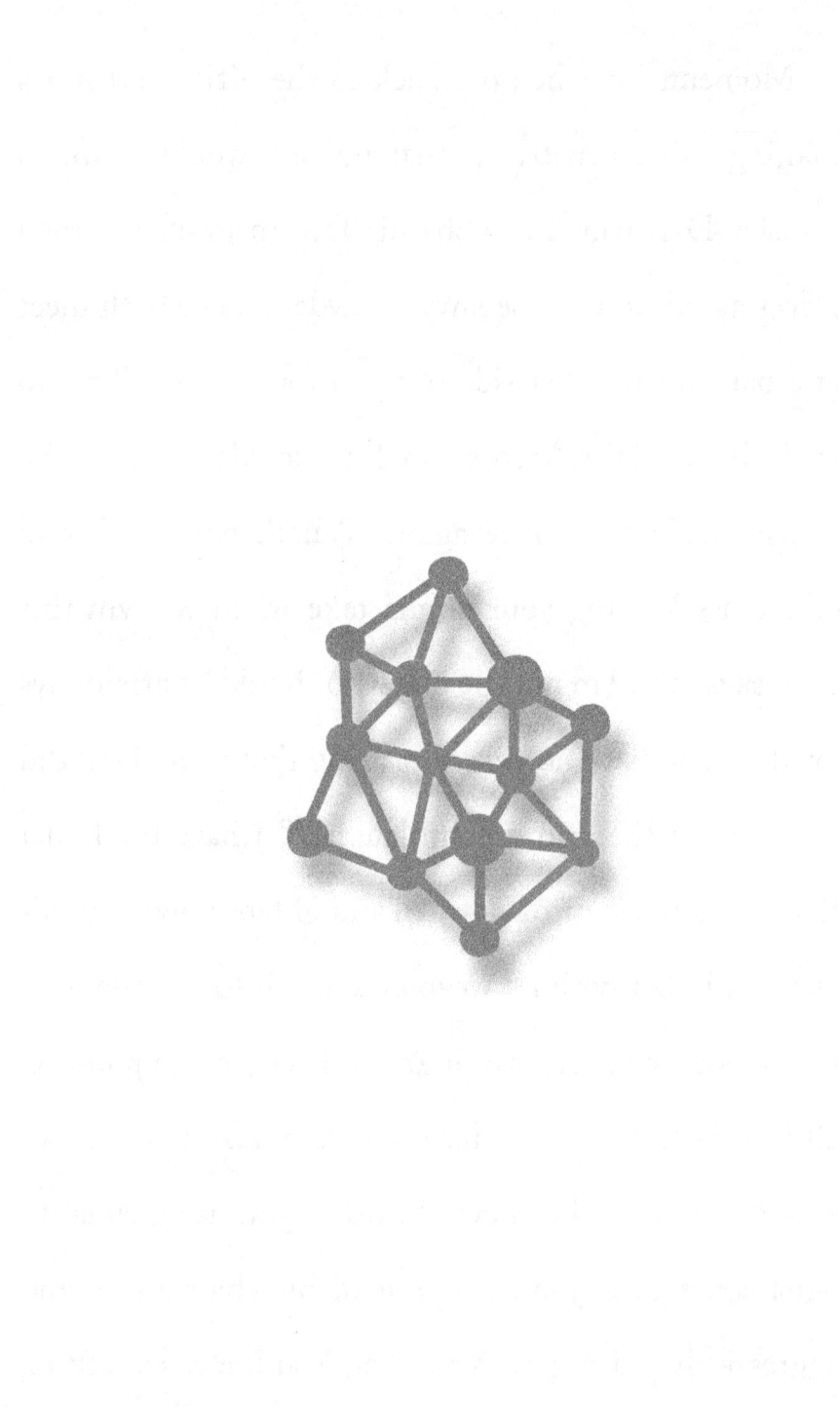

me winning maybe slim to none but I'm gonna beat this case and when I do, your sorry ass is gonna be fucked and when I fuck you your gonna owe me dinner. John leaves the bar. As he leaves, lowden shouts out sarcastically, "make sure I get desert too peaches!

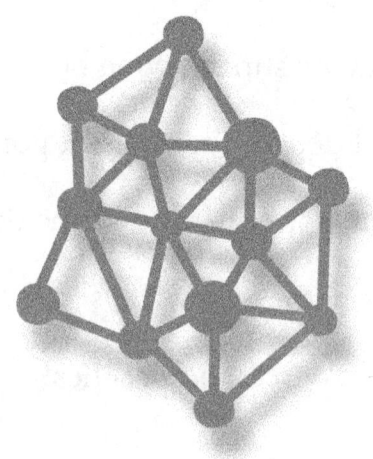

John goes home after a long days work. He is greeted by his beautifully aged wife. Hi, honey she says with her encouraging voice. He sighs expressing how tired and frustrated he is. I see some needs a massage she exclaimed. Oh dear I'm just fighting what most believe is an unwinnable fight. How so? she asked. Well I have a murder suspect who is clearly innocent, but the crime scene proves otherwise. Now I'm gonna be honest, fifteen years ago I would have viewed this as an open and shut case. And now? she replied. "Now with much experience I know better. Now I'm not so sure anymore.Rubbing his shoulders in comfort she says, " Well if I haven't learned anything else from watching you handle your case is that every man deserves a fare trial no matter the crime and out come. sometimes the smallest break in the case could be sitting right in front of you. John Arrises the next morning preparing himself for the first part of trial. He heads over to the jail to briefly talk to Damarius. Hey how's it going son? he asks. Damarius folds his hands

on the recreational table. "I'm maintaining he says. The guards haven't made a move on me participating in any fights, and Santos been in solitaire for two weeks, so I've been good. I think he likes it in their. "Are you ready for today? he asks John. "Yea as ready as I'll ever be....I must warn you though. This is just the beginning the first part. People are gonna say things about you and this case, that you may not agree with. Their gonna try to paint this ugly picture of you as a monster with no regards to human life. But I'm not! shouts Damarius. John goes on to say, " All I ask is that you please contain yourself. I know this judge and she is not friendly. She'll make a conviction with your behavior being just cause and believe you, me she has done it once before.

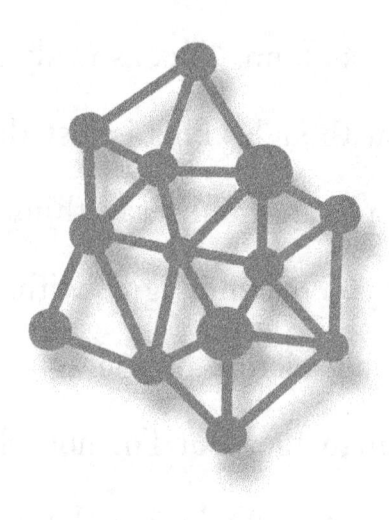

Hours later Damarius is driven to Langburg court house. He is escorted into the court room wrists handcuffed tighter then a age old bracelet. Staring off into the crowded room, he can't help but notice Mr Jay's wife looking back at him with hatred and disgust in her eyes. Come on now stay focus don't let that get to you. "whispers John into his left ear. The guard announces, "All arise the Honorable judge Wade presiding. Judge Wade sits in her chair with such a stern look. Case number 800295 The people vs. Damarius Thomas. says the guard. The judge acknowledges the people in the court room. "Goodmorning everyone. she says. OK shall we began. Mr Thomas, your being accused and charged with first degree murder of Mr Jay Morgan in which you claim despite the evidence that you are innocent. Is that correct? she asks Damarius. That is correct. he replied. And how do you plead Mr Thomas? she asks. Not guilty your honor. At this time I would like for the defense to call it's first witness. Lowden stands up, showing off his

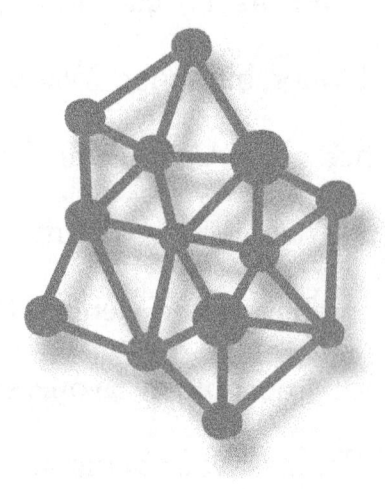

military style hair cut and his JC Penney suit. I'd like to call officer Ryan Gould to the stand. Officer Gould is sworn in. "Tell me what is your position on the force? asks lowden. I am a ten year veteran on the Baltimore city police force. he replied. I've worked the Western district for four years, then in 2005 I was transferred and did six years. lowden begans to say, "So tell me what you have observed or heard on the night of the incident. "Well my partner and I....officer piercing that is, on Mark way. At around 9:30 pm we received an anonymous call of a man screaming in distress. My partner and I went to investigate. When we arrived at the scene, we observed two males. One black male crying and the other black male clearly motionless and deceased. lowden asks with such curiosity, " And what did you do? . Officer Gould replies, " I began to radio for emergency assistance as protocol but I could tell their was no need the guy was so limp. I must ask you officer Gould says lowden. Did you observe any other individuals at the scene or surrounding

areas. Gould responds besides the neighborhood on lookers who came to find out what the fuss was, I saw no one who seemed displaced. So in your best opinion officer do you believe the defendant Damarius Thomas committed the crime? asks lowden. Gould responds yes in my best opinion I think he did, the evidence doesn't lie.

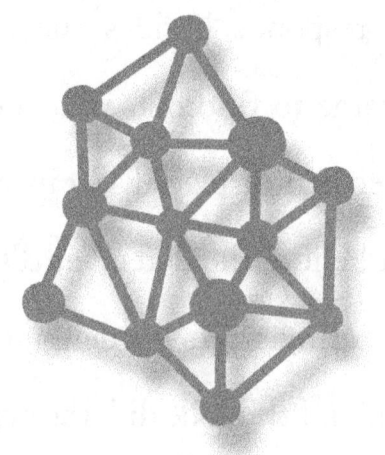

"Nothing further. says Lowden. Your witness says Judge Wade. John gets up. "So you said you saw no one? John questions Gould. Gould replies with certainty, "No not a soul. "So is it not safe to say someone else committed the vicious act? "No it's not possible says Gould. John steps forward and places his hand on the witness stand. "How can you be so sure? It's one of the quiet blocks, which is saying alot considering we live in a high crime city. Besides with that amount of blood contact theirs no doubt in my mind. Damarius breathes heavily out of anger. John laughs, "So your telling me based off the bloody shirt, my client being at the scene, and all arrows pointing to him, that my client is guilty? Gould becomes defensive, "Yes I do, I mean come on you know how they are. John slightly turns his head." They who? he asks. You know them Gould replies. "I don't follow. Gould straightens his body. "You know them. John is appauled, "Are you saying blacks......African Americans? So basically you are implying that just because my client

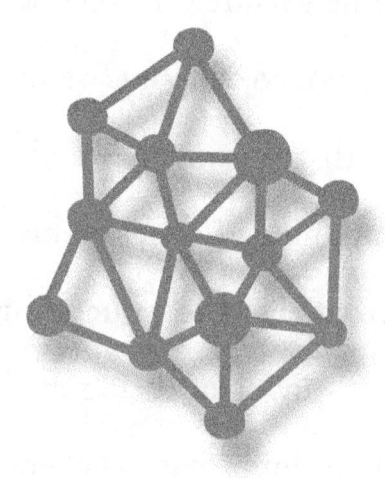

is black and a known drug dealer, he committed the crime? Gould grunt, "They run our streets selling drugs wanting government handouts. If they invested half as much time into positive projects as they do in the streets the city wouldn't be going to shits!!! John is disgusted. Well officer your entitled to your opinion but I must say though your excising your freedom of speech I find your racial bias to be offensive....the defense is done with this witness. Nothing further your honor. Judge Wade goes on to say are their anymore witness's to be presented today? Lowden stands up, " the state rests your honor. "How about you John? she asks. The defense rests. he says. Alright court will adjourn and continue Tuesday morning in which in case Lowden will present the next witness. The gravel bangs. Court is adjourned.

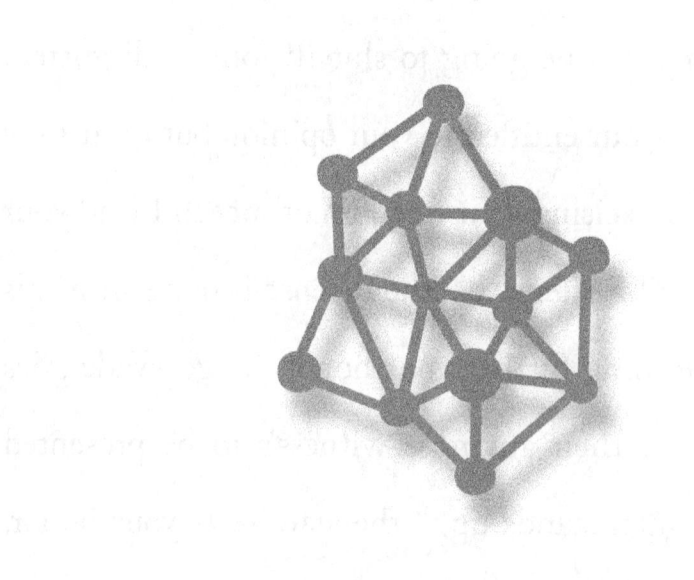

A women hands Lowden a paper. He forms a sneaky grin as if he is pleased at the note given. John is confused considering his witness just took a dive which had given him the upper hand in the case. Lowden walks over to John and shakes his hand. What do you have up your sleeve? John asks. Lowden laughs" I haven't the slightest idea of what your talking about. I just simply wanted to show gratitude. I can be nice....sometimes. Lowden walks away with a smile. Damarius walks over to John. "We did good he says. "Yeah that's what I'm afraid of with this being the beginning, we did way to good. John returns home catching up on some much needed rest. Trying to take his mind off the case for a moment, he could not help but worry. The constant reminder of Lowden's grin is what worried him the most. He takes a long hot bath then offs himself to bed. The next morning he is awakened by the bombastic sounds of his ringtone. Hello? he grunts still trying to adjust to the morning son piercing through his window." Hey John, says his assitant,

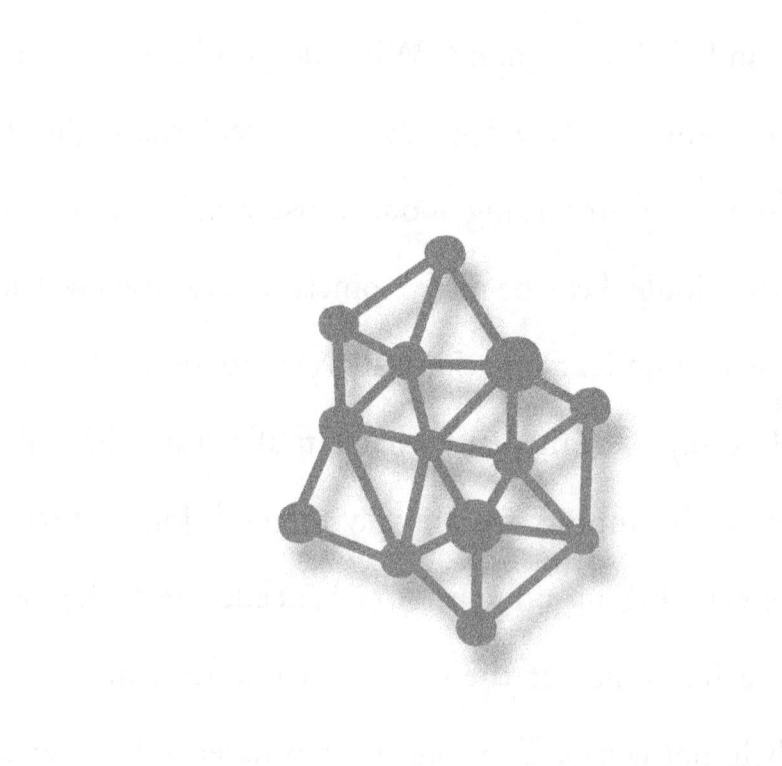

attorney Micheal miles. We have a huge problem. "Yeah, What could be the problem says John. The bullet you found, is not being admitted as evidence. It's not being tested either. The judge threw it out John. he says.John scoweled in fiery, " What do you mean she threw it out. "I'm on my way, you tell Taylor to hang on to that bullet. His career is riding on it. John rushes to the court house. He spots the judge in the hallway. As she diverse with another judge, John stops the conversation. What the fuck is your problem? he screams.

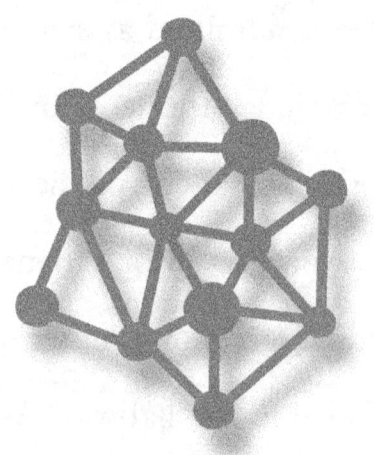

Do you not like me? or are you living in a fantasy world on planet idiot.She sternly shouts out, " Excuse me Mr John Tucker! That type of language will not be tolerated in this court house. In my chambers immediately!. John follows behind still enraged. Now What seems to be the problem that you feel the need to storm the court house like a ragging bafoon. John rubs the back of his head. "Your dismissing the only piece of evidence that may or may not give my client his freedom....why? Taking a seat in her chair, Judge Wade replied, "I had to, clearly you haven't reviewed the fact of the case. Unless we have a weapon to pin it to with prints, we have nothing. We can use it but how will we find a killer. Without the gun the, the bullet is as good as as hear say. Not to mention it could be argued that the bullet could have come from any gun based off the crime rate in this city. John laughs sarcastically, "this is insane. John returns to the jail greatly disappointed. "Aye what's going on? Damarius says in joy. John taps his hand on the table briefly procrastinating on

a response. "Their not presenting the bullet as evidence.... Judge says theirs no weapon to match it so it's not admissible in court. "What do you mean? he whimpers. "I know says John but the defense can argue that it could have come from any gun, it could have been planted, or it was left from a previous encounter. Either way we are screwed, hell they won't even run tests against the body and the bullet residue. John sighs in pity....I don't know. Damarius grabs John by the shoulder. Listen don't give up hope. I believe I was innocent. whether we win or not, you did your best. John began to tear up enough for Damarius to notice. He knew that in his heart the fight would be great and a lost of this magnitude would crush his spirit. He was not prepared to look a innocent man in the eye and say hey I did my best but your still going do life for another man's crime.

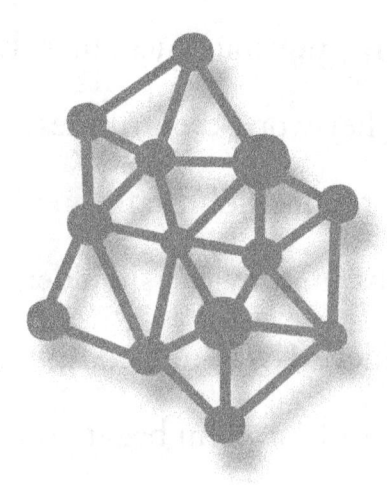

The days go by as they go through a constant battle in court, arguing and trying to prove Damarius's innocence. Even though he fought hard, Lowden and his team were prepared for everything the defense was throwing at them. After a tough week, John retired to his den with a huge bottle of scotch in his hand. Drinking from the bottle and gazing at the fireplace. His wife enters observing the frustrated Mr Tucker. "Hey honey" Are you okay? she asked. "We' re gonna lose you know? in all my years I've never felt like such a big fat failer until now. "Your not a failer "she exclaimed. Just because you've lost the battle dosent mean you'll lose the war. The final judgment is tommarrow, but you still have plenty of time to prove his innocence. John sits forward in his chair. I know but it just doesn't sit right knowing that he may spend the rest of his life in prison, for a crime he didn't commit. I do know one thing though. If I lose lowden won't let me hear the end of it.

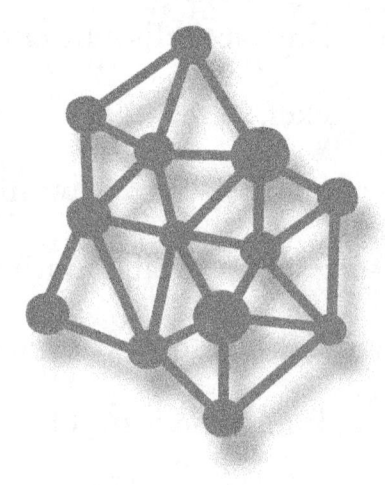

The cool morning comes with a cold chill of mystery in the air. Everyone is nervous about the unknown turnout of the case. One last argument, one last chance to convince a jury of his peers, that he is not guilty of the haynous crime. John meets lowden in the hallway of the court house. Lowden shakes his hand. "Good luck in court today John. he says."

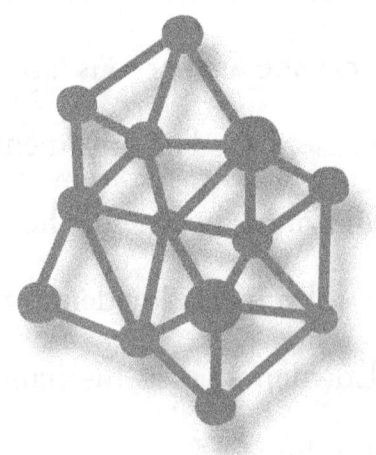

Thanks Lowden he replies still skeptical. They enter the court room with such weight on their shoulders. Damarius looks around realizing since the case has blown up in the news, the media is watching and the audience has grown tremendously in size. The jury carefully examines him. He could tell by the looks on their faces, they were voicing their opinions of him silently in their own heads. The guard announces." All rise, the Honorable judge Wade presiding. "How's everyone good afternoon. This is the final day in which a verdict will be met in this case. Today both sides will be heard in which in case after all witness testimony is heard and all evidence is presented. The jury will retire and then return with a verdict. If the jury cannot reach one do to a split decision, then majority rule will be considered. If it's evenly split, then I would have no choice but to throw it out. The plaintiff may call it's first witness.Lowden stands up. I call Mr Eric Porter to the stand. Curve takes the stand sworn in promising to tell the truth. Lowden approaches the

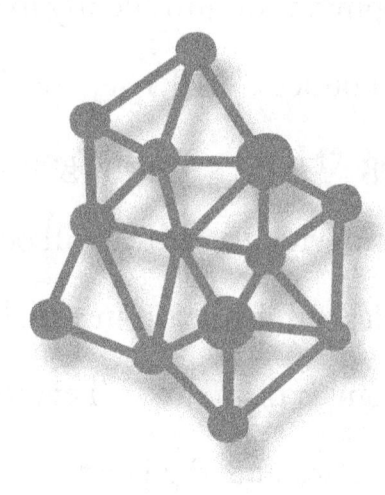

witness. stand. "Tell me Mr Porter" You previously stated that Mr Thomas does not or did not have any violent tendicies. That even though he acts mean and like a thug, he's not violent correct? That's correct he acknowledges. "You said if anything your the one that's violent." Yes sir. says curve. "I wonder. Tell me Mr Porter, how is it that a person could be around another individual majority of his life and not display not even a hint of violence. "Well I'm not a mind reader sir. Everyone reacts differently to different circumstances and situations. The jury Chuckle's. Lowden further explains, " well I have witness testimony that in fact after a run in with a known gang member, he actually punched the guy knocking him into the potato chip stand. Curve becomes defensive. "Well just because he punched a guy, dosent make him a violent person." I disagree Mr Porter, says Lowden. Physical contact resulting in injury or harm is one of the main signs of violent behavior. A man capable of violence is a man capable of murder. Curve looks at Damarius then

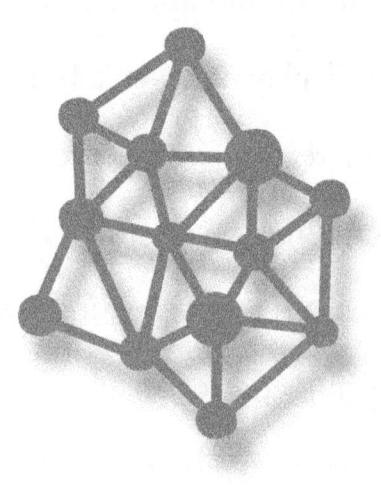

at Lowden. I mean, I'm not saying he can't........Lowden cuts him off. Cornering his every word. Your lying under earth Mr Porter, he says. Previously you've given witness testimony that this man Damarius Thomas, your long time friend had no violent tendicies, yet he gathered up enough anger to punch a rival gang member. Not just hard enough to hurt him but so hard he knock him into a chip stand. Now I don't know if you know the true meaning of the word violence but in my book that was a violent act. Eric Sat in his chair dumb founded and speeches. Lowden replies, " Nothing further your honor. "Any questions for this witness, she asks. "No questions, says John. John gets nervous. After his key witness gets grilled to the point of being stumpt, he thinks about withdrawing from the case. Damarius See's the defeated expression on his face and stares at him with hope and reassurance." Next witness. judge Wade Insists. "The defense calls Marget Geddy to the stand.

Lowden quickly gets out of his seat." I object your honor this witness was not on the list! John quickly fires back, " The state had been notified of this witness and was given ample time to question and examine this witness, however they did not follow up on procedure to do so. "I'll allow this witness testimony but I suggest you make it count John. Lowden sits down slowly puzzled. "So Mrs Geddy can you please state your name and your place of residence. "Well I'm Margret Geddy and I live two houses across from the alley. "Ok and can you tell me what you saw on the night in question? asks John. Mrs Geddy replies, " Well I was watching family fued around eight. I heard gun shots, a man crying. Moments later is when you guys showed up. Did you see anything out of the ordinary prior to the shooting that day? "It seemed like a normal day except a few dressy men coming out of the store. "Did these men seem threatening or look odd? "Well no they looked like regular dressed men. "Nothing further your honor". The judge turns to Lowden." Your

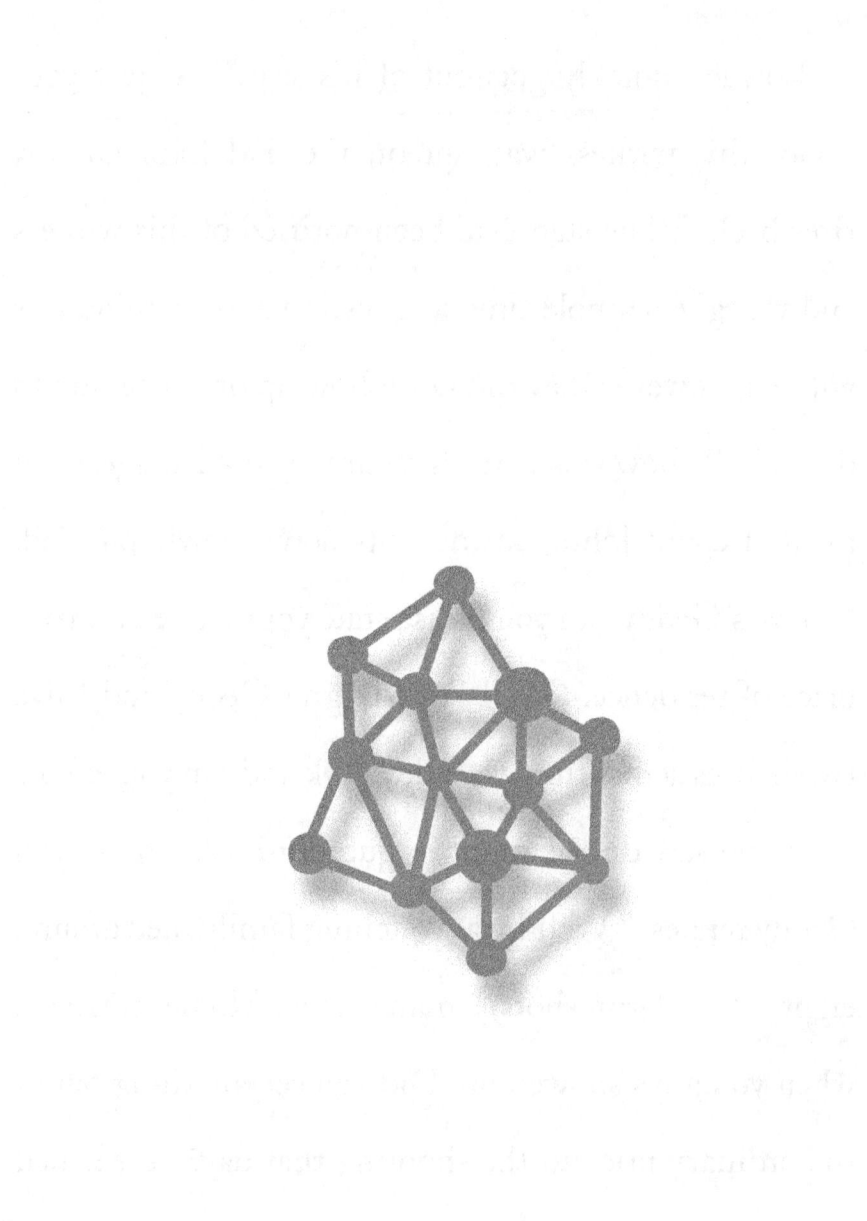

witness, she says. Lowden begans to question. "Mrs Geddy, you indicate that you saw some well dressed me leave the store correct? "That is correct she agreed. Now in such a neighborhood isn't it odd that on a day other then Sunday, three well dressed men enter a store." Well I suppose so. she said. "In fact from the angle of your house, you can see pretty much half way through the alley. I'm curious. I'm curious because in your sworn statement you said you heard shots fired but you didn't call the police, why is that. "Well I was going to But I was distracted by the car that drove off. she replied. "What car? he asked. "A dark colored car drove off but before it did a Young man looked up at me then got in the car.

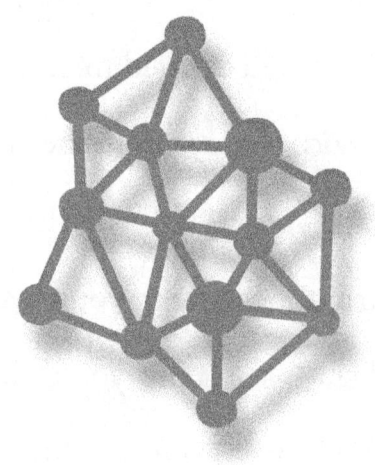

Lowden is enlightened by this new information. "Did you get a good look at this person? he asked. "Yes he stood under the street light as if he wasn't trying to hide his face. she said nervously. "Who was the man? said Lowden. "The young man sitting directly behind Mr Damarius Thomas. Eric Porter aka Curve tries to flee the court room. "Apprehend him! yells judge Wade. Curve is forcefully put on the witness stand and sworn under oath. Lowden begins to question. "Did you Eric Porter murder Mr Jay? . "You don't know what type of hood I grew up in. Did you murder Mr Jay Mr Porter? "Drugs, poverty, police shootings, crackheads, little to no money. "Goddamit Mr Porter did you murder Mr Jay? Curve gets emotional and screams out, "All he had to do is fucking sell! We offered him big money. The people of the court gasps and quiet strikes the room. He looked at the check in such disgust, spit in it and after balling it up said he couldn't be bought. Lowden asks, " but why Damarius why frame your best friend. Curve slouches

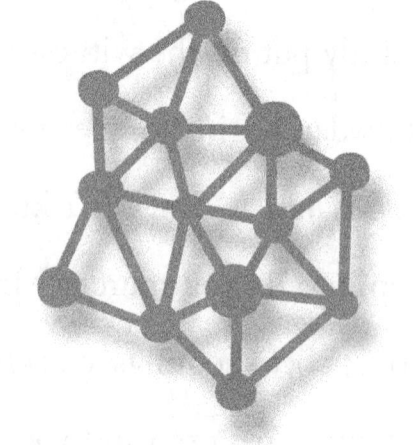

back in his seat. "Survival of the fittest we were going set up a new drug house calculated to profit millions of dollars. Damarius was the top dog for years and I got tired of standing in his shadow. Everybody in the streets know if you want the money power and respect, you gotta get rid of the top dog. I figured I'd murder Mr Jay, let Damarius take the rap and in the end be on top. It happened so perfectly. With me being the head of the hillen burg niggas, that's all I needed. "You switched sides mothafucka!!! I thought we was cool, I thought we was boys!! screamed Damarius. Lowden turns to John." Your witness. John rises out of his seat. You have the right to remain silent anything you say will be used against you in the court of law.You have the right to an attorney, if you can't afford one, one will be appointed to you. Do you understand these rights as they have been read to you? Curve was taken into custody.

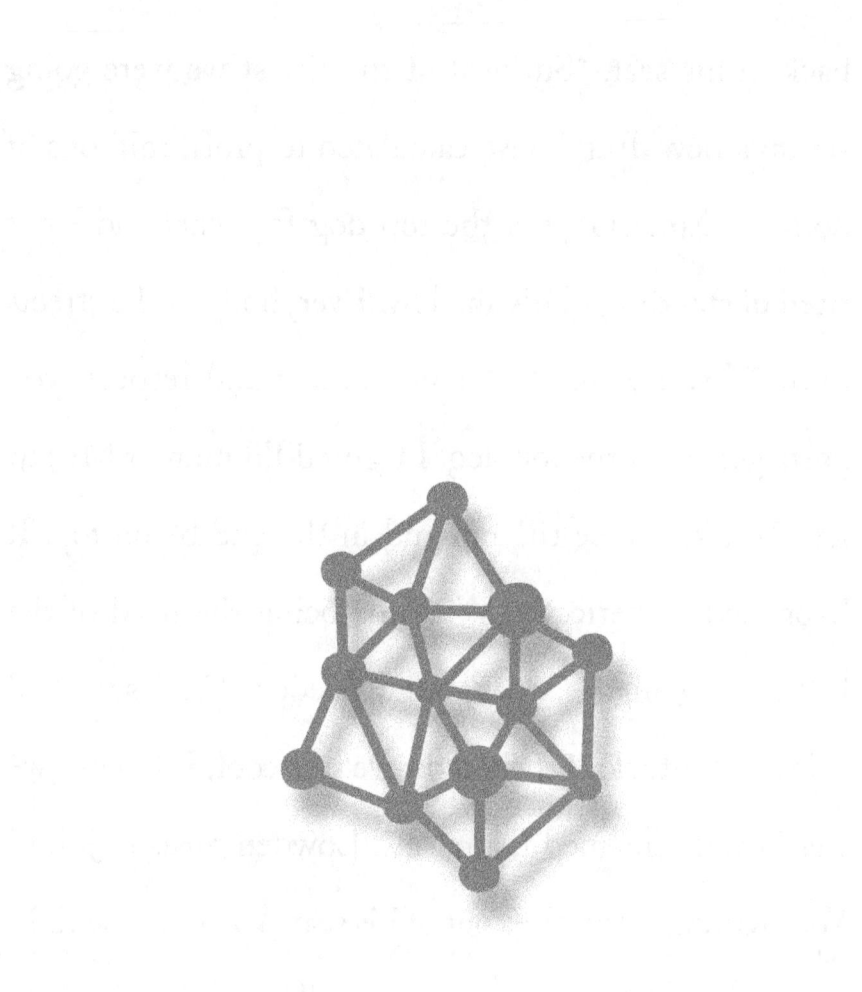

Damarius turns to John. "We did it, we did it. John replies, " Yes we did. Damarius was released as a free man. He started a family with a childhood friend and enrolled in college fall classes. Curve was sentence to Life in prison without the possibility of parole. Lowden died after a massive heart attack. John left the law firm and retired in Hawaii. In honor of Mr Jay, he wrote a book. It was based on the perspectives of all parties invoved in the case and Showed both points of view both brown and blue.

CPSIA information can be obtained
at www.ICGtesting.com
Printed in the USA
BVHW031031160519
548478BV00004B/32/P